Highland Sam J. Racadio & ELC

7863 Central Avenue
Highland, CA 92346

Welcome to ALADDIN QUIX!

If you are looking for fast, fun-to-read stories with colorful characters, lots of kid-friendly humor, easy-to-follow action, entertaining story lines, and lively illustrations, then **ALADDIN QUIX** is for you!

But wait, there's more!

If you're also looking for stories with tables of contents; word lists; about-the-book questions; 64, 80, or 96 pages; short chapters; short paragraphs; and large fonts, then **ALADDIN QUIX** is *definitely* for you!

ALADDIN QUIX: The next step between ready to reads and longer, more challenging chapter books, for readers five to eight years old.

**Read the other book
in the Elf Academy series!**

Trouble in Toyland

Elf ACADEMY

REINDEER GAMES

BY ALAN KATZ

ILLUSTRATED BY
SERNUR IŞIK

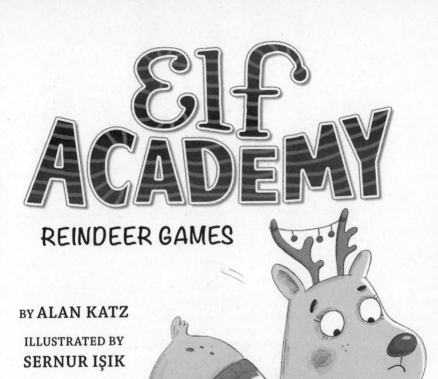

ALADDIN QUIX

NEW YORK LONDON TORONTO SYDNEY NEW DELHI

ALADDIN QUIX

Simon & Schuster Children's Publishing Division

1230 Avenue of the Americas, New York, New York 10020

First Aladdin QUIX hardcover edition February 2022

Text copyright © 2022 by Simon & Schuster, Inc.

Illustrations copyright © 2022 by Sernur Işik

Also available in an Aladdin QUIX paperback edition.

For information about special discounts for bulk purchases, please contact Simon & Schuster Special Sales at 1-866-506-1949 or business@simonandschuster.com.

The Simon & Schuster Speakers Bureau can bring authors to your live event. For more information or to book an event contact the Simon & Schuster Speakers Bureau at 1-866-248-3049 or visit our website at www.simonspeakers.com.

Designed by Tiara Iandiorio

The illustrations for this book were rendered digitally.

The text of this book was set in Archer Medium.

Manufactured in the United States of America 1221 LAK

2 4 6 8 10 9 7 5 3 1

Library of Congress Control Number 2021941925

ISBN 9781534467927 (hc)

ISBN 9781534467910 (pbk)

ISBN 9781534467934 (ebook)

To the wonderful Newsom family

—A. K.

Cast of Characters

Andy Snowden: An Elf Academy student

Jay: Andy's best friend

Ms. Dow: The toy workshop teacher at Elf Academy

Zahara: An Elf Academy student

Roger: The rancher at Reindeer Ranch

Susu: Andy's twin sister

Kal: An Elf Academy student

Nicole: Susu's best friend

Molly: One of the reindeer at Reindeer Ranch

Wally: One of the reindeer at Reindeer Ranch and twin brother of Molly

C. J.: One of the reindeer at Reindeer Ranch

Eli: One of the reindeer at Reindeer Ranch

Christy: One of the reindeer at Reindeer Ranch

Melody: One of the reindeer at Reindeer Ranch

Contents

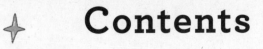

1

The Countdown

Everyone knows that December is a very busy month at the North Pole toy-building workshop.

Last minute details like tying ribbons, sewing buttons, gluing wheels, and painting birdhouses keep the elves **hopping** all day and all night long.

It wasn't until Santa and his reindeer took off for their Christmas Eve flight that the elves felt they could rest.

But making toys wasn't the only job the elves had at Elf Academy.

During the other eleven months of the year they planted trees, **designed** snow sculptures, tasted candy-cane apple pie recipes, and made sure the reindeer were ready for their ride with Santa.

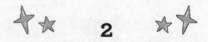

2

And that's what was on **Andy Snowden**'s mind as he stared at the calendar on the classroom wall.

There was one date **circled**: the day that the second graders in Elf Academy would get to visit Santa's reindeer.

Su	Mo	Tu	We	Th	Fr	Sa
	1	2	③	4	5	6
7	8	9	10	11	12	13
14	15	16	17	18	19	20
21	22	23	24	25	26	27
28	29	30	31			

Reindeer Trip

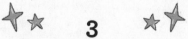

"Our class trip to Reindeer Ranch is in exactly seven days, two hours, nine minutes, and twelve seconds," Andy told his friend **Jay** as he pointed to the clock. **"I can't wait!"**

"No, it's not," Jay said. "It's in seven days, two hours, nine minutes, and *seven* seconds."

"No, it's not," Andy answered. "It's in seven days, two hours, nine minutes, and *two* seconds."

They both laughed.

Ms. Dow, their teacher, overheard the boys, and she laughed too. Then she said, "Actually, you're *both* wrong."

"*We are?*" they asked.

"I'm afraid so," she told them. "The day of the visit has been changed."

"It *has*?" they replied.

"Yes. We are now going to Reindeer Ranch in ten . . ."

"Days?" Andy guessed.

"Weeks?" Jay wondered.

Ms. Dow smiled. "Not quite, Jay. Our class will be going to

Reindeer Ranch in ten . . . minutes.

We are going *today*."

Jay and Andy smiled and yelled,

"Yippee!"

Andy did a triple cartwheel across the workshop, landing in a pile of giant **plush** monster toys the elves had just finished building.

"Are you okay?" Andy's classmate **Zahara** asked.

"Okay? I'm better than okay! **I'm terrific!** After all, we're going to Reindeer Ranch in ten minutes!" The rest of the elves cheered.

"Actually, that's not true," Ms. Dow said. "We're going in nine minutes and forty-seven seconds...."

2

At the Ranch

Reindeer Ranch was one of the most popular places at the North Pole. Of course, seeing reindeer wasn't **unusual** around Elf Academy and its surroundings.

But the reindeer who were at the

ranch chose to be there, as they wanted to discover their magical power to fly!

They knew it would take lots of hard work, but they wanted to travel around the world and help Santa deliver joy, cheer, and gifts.

The ranch was a short walk from Elf Academy. Giant fir trees **towered** above the elves, and Andy always loved looking up at his favorite trees.

"Hey, Jay," he said. "Isn't that a snowy . . . ?"

"Did you just say **SNOW**?" Jay laughed as he threw a snow-ball at Andy.

"Not fair, you caught me off guard." Andy giggled. He quickly made a snowball and tossed it at Jay.

"Don't even think about it, boys," Ms. Dow warned. "There'll be plenty of time for snowball fun *after* school."

The best friends grinned and joined the rest of their classmates in line.

"Welcome to Reindeer Ranch!" Roger the Rancher called out as he greeted the elves. "So glad you could come by."

"Thank you, Roger. We are all very glad to be here," Ms. Dow said.

"Especially *me*!" Andy said as he held out a handful of candy. "I'm Andy. Would you like a gumdrop?"

"No, thank you, Andy," Roger answered.

"Well, okay," Andy told him.

"That's my twin sister, **Susu**, and my friend Jay, and there's **Kal**, and **Nicole**. . . ."

Ms. Dow gently **shushed** Andy, but Roger said he was happy to meet the elves.

"You're twins?" Roger asked Andy and Susu. "We actually have a pair of reindeer twins here on the ranch. Come on, follow me and you can meet them."

Roger led the way across a field to where the reindeer were **grazing**.

"Is it mealtime?" Andy asked.

"For reindeer, it's pretty much *always* mealtime," Roger told him. "Most of them eat more than ten pounds of plants, leaves, and other greens every day."

"That's a lot of food. It's a wonder they can fly!" Ms. Dow noted.

"Well, not *all* reindeer can fly. After all, this is Santa's very special **herd**, and they have unique, magical skills," Roger said. "But guess what—all reindeer across the globe are very speedy. In fact,

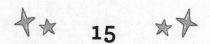

they can run about fifty miles an hour!"

"Wow! That's fast!" the elves said.

Roger then took the class for a close-up look at the reindeer. As they **strolled** through the field, he introduced each reindeer by name.

"This is **Molly** and her twin brother,

Wally. Next are **C. J., Eli, Christy,** and **Melody.**"

"How do the reindeer get their names?" Nicole wondered aloud.

"Believe it or not, they pick them themselves," Roger told her.

"They can *talk*?" Zahara asked.

"Absolutely!" Roger said.

"Yes, if we can fly, don't you think we can talk, too?" Molly said.

"I guess I never thought about that," Zahara said.

Roger explained that just like the elves were learning to be great toy builders, the reindeer were attending classes to be at their best.

"The reindeer take lessons in teamwork, **cooperation**, following directions, maps, and most of all . . . flying," Roger said. "By December 24, they need to be fully prepared to lead Santa's sleigh to homes all around the world."

"How are they doing?" Ms. Dow wanted to know.

"Very nicely," Roger said. "Why don't you all get to know the rein-

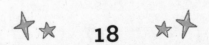

deer better? Each of you should walk around and have a chat with one of them."

The elves couldn't believe their ears. Zahara had a nice talk with Molly.

Susu spoke to Wally.

Kal and C. J. teamed up for a conversation, and so did Jay and Eli. Nicole chatted with Christy.

Lastly, Andy stepped up to Melody and greeted her with a smile.

"Hi," Andy said softly. "Would you like to taste a gumdrop? I've got two pockets full of them."

"**YUCK!** No, thank you," Melody said. "Reindeer don't really like gumdrops. They always get stuck in our teeth,

and it's hard to get them out.
And I'm not in the **mood** for
sweets right now."

Andy asked her if she was
sick. Melody told him she felt

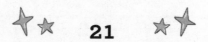

fine. But she did have one problem, and because she was one
of Santa's reindeer, it was a *big*
problem.

"You see, Andy," she whispered.
"I can't fly."

3

Grounded

"What do you mean you can't fly?" Andy asked as he **chomped** on some gumdrops.

"As Roger said, flying takes special, magical skills... and they are skills that I'm afraid I just don't have," Melody answered. She fought back tears.

For once, Andy didn't have a joke or silly story to cheer up Melody.

"Well," he said after a few moments, "the first time I tried to build a scooter, it didn't scoot. The first time I built a rocking horse, it didn't rock."

Andy added, "And the first time I built a sno-cone maker, it didn't make 'sno.' But I kept trying, and after a while, I learned what to do."

He looked at Melody and said,

"Now my scooters always scoot and my rocking horses rock. And you should taste my incredibly delicious sno-cones!"

"That's great, Andy," Melody said. "I'm happy for you. I try and try, but I never **manage** to leave the ground."

"Never?" he asked.

"*Never.* Molly and Wally soar up among the clouds. All the others do too. I just stay right here on earth and watch them fly. So, I have given up," Melody said sadly.

"No!" Andy told her. **"You can't give up!** If my mother has told me once, she's told me a million times: if at first you don't succeed, try, try again!"

"That is a good way of looking at things," Melody said, "and my mama has said the same to me. But as hard as you work in the toy-building workshop, it really doesn't take magic."

Andy was shocked. He didn't know what to say. He was speechless.

Melody continued, "Andy, I think you are very nice. But I have to face the facts. I don't think there's any chance that I'll ever make it into the air."

Just as Melody spoke, she and Andy heard a...

Wh-o-o-o-sh!

★ ★ 27 ★ ★

They saw the other reindeer taking off, each pulling a mini sleigh with an elf inside. There was great laughter in the sky as the reindeer flew higher and higher.

"I'm sorry you picked an **earthbound** reindeer to talk to, Andy," Melody said. "I'm also very sorry I can't take you for a ride like that."

"Don't be sorry," Andy said. "Because I believe that you *can* take me for a ride, and I absolutely believe that you *will* take

me for a ride! **I just know it!**"

Andy was sure Melody would fly one day. But he was also sure he didn't know how it would happen. He wanted to help; he just didn't know how.

4

Magic Time

While his classmates and the other reindeer were soaring above the ranch, Andy led Melody to the open field where the reindeer usually practiced flying.

"Tell me everything you've

learned in flying lessons," Andy said.

"Well," Melody began, "Roger tells us to imagine ourselves flying high."

"And?" Andy asked.

"I do that," Melody said. "I imagine I am in the sky, looking down on Elf Academy and the Clauses' house. And best of all, I imagine I am part of the team that will be delivering toys all around the world."

Andy couldn't help but smile,

and he nodded. Andy had also dreamed of **accompanying** Santa on Christmas Eve. Now, *that* would be a dream come true!

He asked if Roger had given Melody any special words to say before trying to take off.

"Yes," Melody said. "He told me to say three times, 'I can make it to the sky, a jump, a leap, and then I fly!' But I tried **reciting** that and didn't go any-where."

Andy thought for a moment.

"How about taking a running start?" he said.

"I've tried that. Watch me," Melody replied. She took a deep breath, lowered her head, and galloped down the field. Andy could hear her saying,

"I can make it to the sky, a jump, a leap, and then I fly!"

Melody ran faster and faster, but as she zoomed out of sight,

Andy could still hear her hooves—
clippity-clippity-clop—
stomping on the ground. He knew
that meant that she was running,
not flying.

COME BACK!

"Come back, Melody!" Andy shouted. *Wow, she sure did cover a lot of ground in a hurry,* he thought. But too bad it didn't help her take off.

Andy watched as Melody tried again and again, without success. A few minutes later, she slowly and sadly walked back to where he was waiting.

"See, Andy?" she said. "I told you it was no use. You can't deny that I can't fly."

Just then, Molly flew overhead with Zahara in her cart. **"Andy, look at me!"** Zahara called out. "Molly took me to see the polar bears!"

Melody sighed. "That will never be me," she said. "I think I should go and live with the polar bears. Everyone knows they can't fly."

5

Lunch Bunch

One by one the reindeer and the mini sleighs landed, and the elves jumped out, so excited that they were all **chattering** at once.

"That was an awesome ride, Eli," Jay said happily. "Maybe I

can come back next week."

Susu said to Wally, "I'm so glad we're friends."

"Class, over here," Ms. Dow called to them. "Reindeer Ranch is treating us to a special lunch. Each of you will be able to have your meal with your reindeer.

"But remember"—she paused, looking straight at Andy—"you may not eat gumdrops for lunch!"

Everyone laughed, even Andy.

"No problem, Ms. Dow," he answered. "Melody already told

me that they're way too sticky."

The elves quickly lined up for their lunch bags.

"Let's sit over here, Wally," Susu said, pointing to a hill. "Nicole, Christy, come sit with us." Jay and Eli walked over to a group of picnic tables, with Kal and C. J. following.

"Let's hurry up and finish eating so we can all play a game of reindeer and elf soccer," Jay said.

"Well, that's pretty clear, isn't it, Andy?" Melody told him. "The reindeer over there have found their magic, and then there's me. Maybe we should take our lunch somewhere else."

Andy really wanted to play soccer with his friends, but he and Melody trotted over to a nearby barn, painted in all colors of the rainbow.

Wow, Andy thought, *this is serious. Maybe I should tell some jokes? Or try to catch some gumdrops in my mouth with my eyes shut? Will that make Melody feel better?*

"This is one of my favorite spots at the ranch," Melody said, gazing at the barn. "Have you ever seen a *real* rainbow, Andy?"

He nodded. "A couple years ago when I was ice-skating with Susu and my brother, Craig, we saw one that took up the whole sky. Have you?"

"Oh yes," she answered. "I've seen more than I can count. They are so magical."

"Yes, they are!" Andy said, jumping up, his ears starting to **tingle**. "What else do you think is magical, Melody?"

Melody thought for a moment. "I love snowflakes. Did you know that no two are the same? And that reindeer eyes are gold in summer, but turn blue in winter? That's sort of magical too."

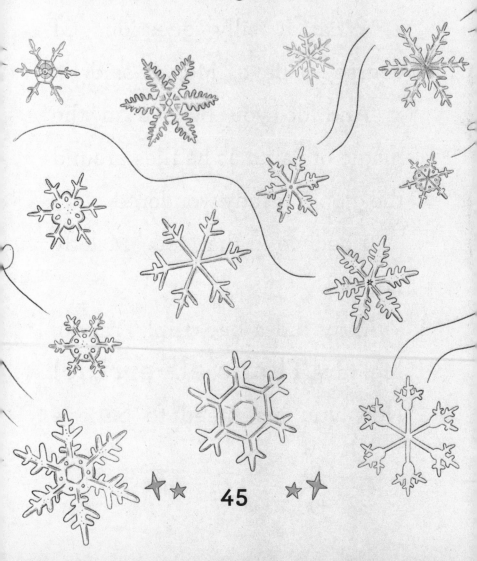

"It sure is! Well, how about Christmas? Do you believe in the magic of Christmas?" Andy asked.

"What a silly question. Of course I believe," Melody said.

"And do you believe in the magic of Santa as he flies around the globe?" Andy wondered.

"I believe in that, too." Melody nodded.

Andy did a backflip! "Yahoo, Melody! **That's elf-errific!** Now you just need to believe that *you* are part of that magic. *You* are part of what makes Santa able to deliver toys to everyone."

"*I am?*" Melody asked him.

"Yes, you *are*," Andy **confirmed**. "Without reindeer like you, the sleigh can't fly, and Santa can't deliver all the toys. You have to believe in the magic that *you* help create."

"I never really thought about it that way before, Andy," Melody said. "I guess it's worth a try."

6

Goody Gumdrops!

Melody stood up. She shook herself off, started to run, and then stopped in her tracks.

She looked back at Andy. "Please say Roger's words with me, okay?"

Andy grinned. "Sure," he told her, "but how about if we say *this* instead?

"Each of us has magic
in our heart;
believing in it is
just the start."

Before Melody could even finish singing, she lifted up off the ground and flew a few feet into the air.

"Andy, is this real?" she asked.

"Am I actually flying?"

Andy quickly ran over to the other elves.

"Look up! Look at Melody! She's done it! She's flying!" he announced, and pointed to the sky. Everyone watched as Melody started soaring high among the clouds.

When Melody finally touched down, the other reindeer excitedly greeted her.

"That was incredible, Melody!" Christy said. "You

look like you've been flying for-ever!"

Andy didn't know reindeer could blush, but he was sure Melody was blushing with happiness. She looked at Andy and winked.

"Well," Roger said, walking over to the group, "this has been a very special day. Thank you all for coming. Before you head back to Elf Academy, I'd like to say an extra thank-you to Andy."

"Really?" Ms. Dow asked him. "What did he do?"

Roger explained that until that day, Melody didn't think she would ever fly.

"But then she met Andy," he

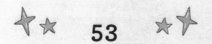

added. "And now I'm pretty sure she will be able to join the other reindeer and help Santa make his next Christmas Eve flight."

"Three cheers for Andy!" Nicole said.

"No, *six* cheers for Andy!" Melody said. "Three from the elves, and three more from the reindeer!"

The elves yelled, **"Hooray! Hooray! Hooray!"** And they clapped their hands, while the reindeer stomped their hooves.

Andy thanked Melody—and everyone else—for the very kind cheers. Melody said that she was glad to show her appreciation for her new friend.

"And do you know what, Andy?" Melody said. "I have one more way to say thank you."

"You do?" Andy asked.

"Yes," she said. "You said that you were sure I'd be able to take you for a ride. Well, thanks to you, now I can."

"Right now?" he asked.

Melody nodded.

"Super!" Andy said. "Ms. Dow, would that be okay?"

"Absolutely, Andy," his teacher said.

In a flash, Melody and Andy were soaring high above Reindeer Ranch.

"See?" Andy said to Melody as they breezed across the sky. "You were able to fly because you believed in the magic of Christmas."

"That may be true, Andy," she

answered. "But *this* flight was possible because I believed in a different kind of magic too."

"A different kind?" Andy wondered.

"Yes," Melody answered. **"The magic of *friendship*."**

At that moment, Andy realized three things:

1. Friendship is a **precious** gift.

2. The trip to Reindeer Ranch had turned out to be everything he hoped it would be.

3. When you're flying up high on a friendly reindeer, you've got to zip up your pockets, or else all your gumdrops will fall down to earth.

That is indeed what happened.

The gumdrops looked like rainbow sparkles in the sky as they dropped into the hands of Andy's friends, just like magic.

It was a delightfully colorful, deliciously sweet surprise for those on the ground.

And as Melody and Andy soared higher and higher, Andy happily called out, "Merry gumdrops to all, and to *me* a good flight!"

Andy & Melody

Word List

accompanying (uh•COM•puh•nee•ing): Going somewhere with someone

chattering (CHA•tur•ing): Speaking quickly or rapidly

chomped (CHOMPT): Bit down on something

circled (SUR•culd): With a loop drawn around it

confirmed (con•FURMD): Told someone that something happened; made certain

**cooperation
(co•ah•puh•RAY•shun):** Working
together to do something

designed (dee•ZINED): Made
plans to create something

earthbound (URTH•bownd):
Limited to the earth; not able to
fly or go to outer space

grazing (GRAY•zing): Eating
grass or plants that grow in a field

herd (HURD): A group of
animals that live together

hopping (HAH•ping): Very
active or busy

manage (MEH•nij): To succeed in doing something

mood (MEWD): The way someone feels

plush (PLUSH): Made of thick, soft fabric

precious (PRE•shus): Greatly loved or valued

reciting (re•SITE•ing): Reading or repeating from something else

shushed (SHUSHD): Told someone to be quiet

strolled (STROLD): Walked slowly

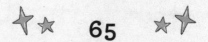

tingle (TEEN•gull): Feel excited

towered (TOW•urd): Stood high
above others

unusual (un•YOO•zhu•wool):
Rare; not common

Questions

1. Which elves in Ms. Dow's class are twins? Which reindeer are twins?

2. Why shouldn't reindeer eat gumdrops?

3. Why does Melody think a snowflake is magical? What do you think is magical?

4. What other animal would you like to see fly besides a reindeer? Would you take a ride?

5. What have you "tried, tried again" to do that you weren't able to do the very first time?